The SCIENCE in Folklore and Proverbs

Dear Reader

People have observed patterns and phenomena in their environments for thousands of years – and often, this knowledge of the natural world has been passed on in the form of folklore and proverbs. Traditional sayings and stories could help farmers predict the weather and care for their animals, keep seafarers and their ships safe from dangerous weather, and explain many of the natural cycles that people in past times relied upon for food, shelter and making decisions about the future.

> “RED SKY IN THE MORNING, SHEPHERD'S WARNING, RED SKY AT NIGHT, SHEPHERD'S DELIGHT.”

Much of this traditional knowledge can be explained by science and, not surprisingly, we now know a great deal of it is based on fact. This book is a fun way of testing your knowledge of some of these traditional sayings – and perhaps learning one or two other useful pieces of folklore along the way. Have fun!

John Parsons

NELSON
CENGAGE Learning™
For learning solutions, visit **cengage.com.au**

Contents

The SCIENCE in Folklore and Proverbs

This book provides instructions for a game, which makes it a procedure. It has been written in the form of a Reader's Theatre text.

Index and Glossary page 32

Aim of the Game

Be prepared for a fun, fast-paced competition, with furious head-scratching and fascinating facts! This is not just another science book – and it's not just another reader's theatre book, either, where characters take turns to read their lines.

It's an interactive, page-turning game that aims to provide the scientific basis behind many of folklore's proverbs. The best part is that no one – not you, not your classmates, not even your teacher – will know what will happen until the very end.

This is a live-action quiz competition for the whole class. But, like all quizzes, preparation is the key. Before you get started, you'll need to have a few props on hand and to familiarise yourself with the rules of the competition.

Characters

You will need the following characters, who can be boys or girls, students or teachers (except the teams, which are not allowed any adults in them):

- QUIZMASTER
- SCRUTINEER
- TIMEKEEPER
- ADJUDICATOR
- TEAMS – made up of four students, one of whom is the team scribe.

The Quizmaster

The quizmaster is the person responsible for narrating the background to each saying or proverb, and for posing the questions that each team must answer. The quizmaster should stand at the front of the class and speak in a clear voice. He or she must also keep the quiz questions coming at a fast pace, so that teams don't have too long to finalise their answers.

The Scrutineer

The scrutineer sits at the desk next to the timekeeper. At the end of each round, each team hands in their answers to the scrutineer, who keeps an accurate record of how many questions each team has answered correctly.

The Teams

Teams are made up of four students. Each team should think up a clever name for themselves, such as “the Scientific Superstars” or “the “Magnificent Mythicals”. One member from each team should be chosen as the person responsible for writing each answer down and handing it in to the scrutineer. This person shall be known as the team scribe.

The Timekeeper

The timekeeper sits at the desk next to the adjudicator. After each question is posed by the quizmaster, the timekeeper uses their watch or clock to allow 30 seconds for each team to write down their answer. To add to the pressure, the last ten seconds must be counted down aloud!

The Adjudicator

The adjudicator is the person who reveals the correct answers after all the teams have handed in their answer slips to the scrutineer.

Props

You will need the following props:

- The adjudicator, timekeeper and scrutineer will need a desk or table at the front of the class to sit at.
- The timekeeper will need a watch or a clock with a second hand on it.
- The scrutineer will need a pen, a pad or sheet of paper and a whiteboard and marker pen.
- Each team will need a desk or table to sit around.
- The team scribe will need a pen and three sheets of paper, one for each round.

Rules of the Science in Folklore and Proverbs Quiz

During the quiz, only the quizmaster, the adjudicator and the scrutineer are allowed to have copies of this book open.

Text in the green boxes is not for speaking out loud.

There will be three rounds of three questions.

At the start of each round, each team must write their team name clearly at the top of a piece of paper. After the quizmaster poses each question, the teams will have 30 seconds to decide on an answer and write it down. At the end of each round, the answers must be handed to the scrutineer. The scrutineer keeps a record of the number of correct answers each team gives and, at the end of the quiz, he or she will announce the top teams.

If a team submits an answer that is unclear, the adjudicator will decide whether the given answer is correct or incorrect.

THE MOST IMPORTANT RULE:

IF YOU'RE A MEMBER OF A TEAM, AND YOU'RE PLAYING IN THIS QUIZ,

CLOSE YOUR COPY OF THIS BOOK NOW!

The **Science** in Agricultural Folklore and Proverbs

QUIZMASTER:

Welcome, teams, to our science in folklore and proverbs quiz! Before we start the quiz, if anyone has a copy of this book open on their desks, please close it now.

First, I'd like each team to introduce themselves. As I point to each team, the team scribe will stand and announce their team's name to the rest of the class.

(The quizmaster points to each team, one after the other, and allows each team scribe to reveal their team's name.)

Thank you, teams. Now, I'd like each team scribe to write the name of their team at the top of a piece of paper, and get ready to write down their answers to this round of questions.

Are you all ready? Then let the quiz commence! This first round is about folklore and proverbs in agriculture.

Question 1

QUIZMASTER:

A common saying for something that happens very rarely is "once in a blue moon". But just how often does a blue moon appear?

Is it:

(a) never

(b) approximately once every hundred years

(c) approximately once every two-and-a-half years?

Thirty seconds, teams. Write down your answer: a, b or c.

TIMEKEEPER:

(waits until 20 seconds have passed, then counts down the last ten seconds):

10. 9. 8. 7. 6. 5. 4. 3. 2. 1.

Native American Moon Names

Folklore Fact

The northern Native American Algonquin tribes gave each monthly moon a different name.

January	Full Wolf Moon
February	Full Snow Moon
March	Full Crow Moon
April	Full Pink Moon
May	Full Flower Moon
June	Full Strawberry Moon
July	Full Buck Moon
August	Full Sturgeon Moon
September	Full Corn Moon
October	Full Hunter's Moon
November	Full Beaver Moon
December	Full Cold Moon

Question 2

QUIZMASTER:

When people are tempted to criticise a gift they have been given, they are often warned not to "look a gift horse in the mouth". This means it is considered ungrateful to try and work out how valuable a gift is. But why would someone have wanted to look into a horse's mouth to try and work out how valuable it was?

Is it:

(a) because they wanted to see what the horse had been eating

(b) because they wanted to see what the horse's teeth looked like

(c) because they wanted to see if the horse had a sore throat?

Thirty seconds, starting now! Write down your answer: a, b or c.

TIMEKEEPER:

(waits until 20 seconds have passed, then counts down the last ten seconds):

10. 9. 8. 7. 6. 5. 4. 3. 2. 1.

Question 3

QUIZMASTER:

If someone is called "the black sheep of the family", it is often meant as a criticism. It implies that the person doesn't behave as the other members of the family do, and that their behaviour may cause problems. This saying arose because in the old days, farmers were disappointed when a black sheep was born into a flock of white sheep. Why would the appearance of a black sheep in a flock of white sheep have been a problem for farmers?

Is it:

(a) because few people wanted black wool

(b) because black sheep were usually more badly behaved than white sheep

(c) because if a black sheep bred with a white sheep, any resulting sheep would have had grey wool?

Thirty seconds, teams, to write your answer down: a, b or c.

TIMEKEEPER:

(waits until 20 seconds have passed, then counts down the last ten seconds):

10. 9. 8. 7. 6. 5. 4. 3. 2. 1.

That's the end of Round One, teams. Now, all team scribes must hand in their answers to the scrutineer.

(Once all teams have handed in their answer sheets, the adjudicator stands. While the quizmaster and the adjudicator are giving the following answers, the scrutineer counts up the correct answers for each team and records the results on the whiteboard.)

QUIZMASTER:

Answer to question 1: How often does a blue moon appear?

ADJUDICATOR:

Until the start of modern agricultural practices, around a century ago, most farmers planted and harvested their crops according to the seasons and the phases of the moon. In most years, three full moons would appear during each of the four seasons, making a total of 12 full moons per year, or one per month. Farmers knew to plant crops before the last full moon of winter, and to harvest them before the last full moon of summer.

But because the orbit of the moon around Earth is not exactly one month, every so often there would be 13 full moons in a year. One of the seasons would end up having an extra full moon. This extra full moon was known as a "blue" moon. Farmers who planted or harvested by the phases of the moon had to be aware of this extra moon, or their schedules would become out of step with the seasons.

A blue moon is actually quite common. There's an extra full moon about once every two-and-a-half years. The correct answer to Question 1 is (c).

Folklore Fact

Ash Before Oak

An old farmers' rhyme is "Ash before oak, the summer's a soak, oak before ash, the summer's but a splash". This meant that if leaves appeared on an ash tree before an oak tree, the summer would be wet. If an oak tree's leaves unfurled first, the summer would have only light rain. Ash trees are light sensitive and unfurl their leaves when the days become longer. Oak trees are heat sensitive and unfurl their leaves when the temperature rises. Therefore, if an oak tree's leaves appear first, the weather is warmer and a hot, dry summer is likely.

an ash tree (left) and an oak tree (right)

Answer to question 2: Why would someone have wanted to look into a horse's mouth to try and work out how valuable it was?

ADJUDICATOR:

In the old days, the value of a horse depended on how old it was. A young horse, fit and full of energy, was much more valuable to a farmer than an old horse, which was more likely to be tired and less able to work hard.

An experienced farmer could accurately tell the age of a horse by examining its teeth. Like humans, horses have milk teeth, or "baby teeth", and permanent teeth, which are larger and stronger. A horse gets its permanent two front teeth at the age of three years. Permanent teeth replace milk teeth on either side of the front teeth at four years of age. At five years of age, the next two teeth on either side appear.

A horse's permanent teeth have deep hollows, or "cups", on their surface. By the time a horse is over ten years old, most of these hollows will have been ground away through the action of chewing fibre, soil or sand. The age of a horse between six and ten years old can be estimated by how deep the "cups" in its teeth are.

The age of a horse's teeth can also be deduced by their shape. A young horse has broad, flat teeth. By the age of ten years, the back surface of each tooth will have been ground into an oval shape. By the time a horse is around 15 years old, the back surface of its teeth will almost always be triangular.

The answer to Question 2 is (b): because the person wanted to see what the horse's teeth looked like as a way of assessing the horse's age and ability to work.

Folklore Fact

Long in the Tooth

If someone is described as being "long in the tooth", it means they are old. This saying came about because horses' teeth, unlike human teeth, keep growing as the horse gets older. A horse with long teeth will be older than a horse with short teeth.

A foal has very short teeth.

An older horse has very long teeth.

Strike While the Iron's Hot

This is another common saying that means "act quickly when an opportunity arises". Blacksmiths, who make horseshoes and other iron implements, knew the best time to shape iron was to hit or strike it when it was red-hot. This is because, at high temperatures, the atoms in metals can slide past each other without breaking.

a blacksmith shapes a red-hot horseshoe

White or Black?

Science Fact

If a sheep's mother and father contribute one gene each to their offspring, there are four ways the genes can combine. But, as a white gene will always cancel out a black gene, only one combination will result in a black sheep:

QUIZMASTER:

Answer to question 3: Why would the appearance of a black sheep in a flock of white sheep have been a problem for farmers?

ADJUDICATOR:

Wool colour is determined by a sheep's genetic makeup, which it inherits from its parents. White wool is determined by dominant genes and black wool is determined by recessive genes. If a sheep inherits both dominant and recessive genes from its parents, then the dominant genes cancel out the recessive genes and the sheep has white wool.

Before today's distinctive breeds of sheep were developed using careful genetic selection, around one in 20 sheep could be born with black wool, making them relatively common.

However, black wool could not be dyed as easily as white wool, and the demand for black wool for use in fabrics was limited. A farmer would have been disappointed when he saw a black sheep in his flock because he knew he wouldn't make any money from its wool.

The answer to Question 3 is (a): because few people wanted black wool.

SCRUTINEER:

The results of round one are as follows. *(The scrutineer announces each team's scores.)*

Round 2

The **Science** in Weather Folklore and Proverbs

QUIZMASTER:

Team scribes, remember to write your team's name at the top of a new piece of paper before you answer these questions. This second round is about the science in weather folklore and proverbs.

Question 4

QUIZMASTER:

Proverbs about the weather derive from long ago when people started observing the weather patterns around them. One of the best-known sayings, which has been told in various forms for over 2 000 years, refers to the colour of the sky at sunrise and sunset: "Red sky in the morning, shepherd's warning, red sky at night, shepherd's delight."

Shepherds were traditionally pleased to see a red sky at sunset because it meant that:

(a) summer was coming

(b) the next day would bring fine weather

(c) their sheep would be easier to see before nightfall.

Which is it, teams: a, b or c?

a sight to please any shepherd

TIMEKEEPER:

(waits until 20 seconds have passed, then counts down the last ten seconds):

10. 9. 8. 7. 6. 5. 4. 3. 2. 1.

Question 5

QUIZMASTER:

If you were aboard a ship before the start of the nineteenth century, you might have heard your seafaring companions repeating the saying: "Mares' tails and mackerel scales make lofty ships lower their sails."

Did the seafarers mean that:

(a) ships carrying horsehair or oily fish preferred to travel slower than other ships

(b) horsehair and mackerel scales were very light cargoes, so not as many sails were needed to maintain a steady speed

(c) certain types of cloud signified that strong winds were on the way?

What's your answer, teams: a, b or c?

TIMEKEEPER:

(waits until 20 seconds have passed, then counts down the last ten seconds):

10. 9. 8. 7. 6. 5. 4. 3. 2. 1.

Folklore Fact

Batten Down the Hatches

The saying "batten down the hatches", which means prepare yourself for some difficult times ahead, comes from an old seafaring term. Strips of wood, called battens, were nailed around the edges of any hatches on deck during stormy weather. This prevented water spilling into the hatches and sinking the ship.

a "battened" hatch on a ship's deck

Question 6

QUIZMASTER:

A popular saying that originated in the Middle Ages goes, "Cold is the night when the stars shine bright." The question is: do stars shine brighter when the weather is colder?

Answer with "yes" or "no", but beware – it might be a trick question!

TIMEKEEPER:

(waits until 20 seconds have passed, then counts down the last ten seconds):

10. 9. 8. 7. 6. 5. 4. 3. 2. 1.

That's the end of the second round! All team scribes must hand in their answers to the scrutineer now.

(Once all teams have handed in their answer sheets, the adjudicator stands. While the quizmaster and the adjudicator are giving the following answers, the scrutineer counts up the correct answers for each team and records the results on the whiteboard.)

A Ring Around the Moon Means Stormy Weather Soon

Folklore Fact

This is also a saying from the Middle Ages. The ring, or halo, sometimes seen around the moon is created by moonlight passing through ice crystals in high-altitude cirrus clouds. These clouds often precede stormy weather. Some people say that counting the stars within the halo will tell you how many days away the storm is.

an ice halo

QUIZMASTER:

Answer to question 4: Why were shepherds traditionally pleased to see a red sky at sunset?

ADJUDICATOR:

As the sun sets in the west, its light passes through a far greater "slice" of the atmosphere than when the sun is directly overhead. When there is a lot of dust, salt, smoke or pollution in the air, the shorter wavelengths of light, which we see as blue, indigo and violet, get blocked. We see only the longer wavelengths of light, which are red, orange and yellow. They pass around the dust like a wave of water washes around a rock or a wharf pile.

An area of high pressure in the atmosphere tends to squeeze the particles in the air closer together. High pressure usually means fine weather. These observations were used to predict the weather. For example, when a shepherd saw a red sky at sunset, it usually meant that the next day would bring fine weather.

The answer to Question 4 is (b): the next day would bring fine weather.

Red Sunsets

In an area of high pressure, dust particles become squeezed closer together. They block out the shorter blue lightwaves. Only the red, orange and yellow lightwaves reach our eyes, and those are the colours we see in the sunset.

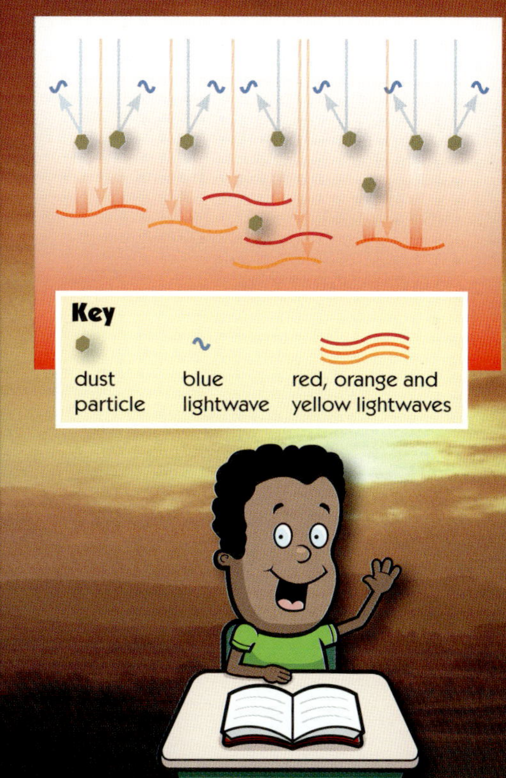

Out of the Blue

Folklore Fact

When something unexpected happens, people say it "came from out of the blue". In old times, this may have referred to blue skies that suddenly turned stormy. But why is the sky blue?

Light travels in waves. Sunlight is made up of different colours of light that all have different wavelengths. Blue light has a short wavelength, so it is easily scattered by gas molecules in the atmosphere. On a clear day, as the light scatters, it appears to be everywhere. On a dusty or cloudy day, however, the smaller blue lightwaves are easily blocked.

QUIZMASTER:

Answer to question 5: What was the meaning of the traditional seafarers' saying that "mares' tails and mackerel scales make lofty ships lower their sails"?

ADJUDICATOR:

In 1803, an English chemist named Luke Howard created the categories of cloud names that we use today. These are: stratus or "layer" clouds, which can cover the entire sky and resemble fog; cumulus or "heaped" clouds, which are puffy with clearly defined edges; cirrus or "wispy" clouds, which are high, thin strands of cloud, and nimbus or "rain" clouds, which are heavy, dark clouds that are full of rain.

mares' tails, or cirrus clouds (above); mackerel scales, or altocumulus clouds (below)

Before these cloud categories were created, people gave names to different kinds of clouds according to how they looked.

Cirrus clouds were known as "mares' tails", because they looked like the strands of a horse's tail. High-altitude cumulus (or altocumulus) clouds were called "mackerel scales", because they looked like a regular pattern of round, pale structures, much like the scales on a fish.

Cirrus clouds (or mares' tails) are made up of ice crystals. Altocumulus clouds (or mackerel scales) are formed through wind changes caused by low-pressure systems. When these two types of cloud are seen together it can mean that a storm is on the way. Sailing ships lowered their sails when a storm was approaching, so that their sails and masts would not be damaged by high winds.

The answer to Question 5 is (c): certain types of cloud signified that strong winds were on the way.

QUIZMASTER:

Answer to question 6: Do stars shine brighter when the weather is colder?

ADJUDICATOR:

Technically, no. Regardless of what the temperature is on Earth, the amount of light emitted by a star will remain unchanged.

However, the amount of moisture in the atmosphere does affect how bright a star may appear to an observer on Earth. Water vapour, in the form of clouds or atmospheric humidity, dims and scatters light that passes through it. This same water vapour also acts as an insulation blanket in the area above Earth where it occurs, trapping heat from Earth's surface.

Therefore, if there is little water vapour to trap Earth's surface heat, that heat will dissipate quickly and it will feel colder. Limited water vapour also means that more light from the stars will reach Earth without being scattered. So, when the night is colder, the stars appear to shine brighter.

The quizmaster warned that this might be a trick question. Because the answer is both "no" and "yes", everyone who answered will get a point for Question 6!

SCRUTINEER:

The results of Round Two are as follows *(announces each team's scores).*

Folklore Fact

Wish Upon A Falling Star

Folklore has it that it is lucky to wish upon a falling star. That is because falling stars were thought to be fairies or angels who had lost their wings and were falling to Earth.

In fact, falling (or shooting) stars are small space rocks called meteoroids, entering Earth's atmosphere and burning up as the friction of the air heats their surface.

The **Science** in Animal Folklore and Proverbs

QUIZMASTER:

Team scribes, remember to write your team's name at the top of a new piece of paper before you answer these questions. This third and final round is about the science in animal folklore and proverbs.

Question 7

QUIZMASTER:

Folklore says that it is possible to work out the exact temperature by listening to a cricket chirping. Is that true, teams? Is a cricket as good as a thermometer? Answer by writing down either "true" or "false".

TIMEKEEPER:

(waits until 20 seconds have passed, then counts down the last ten seconds):

10. 9. 8. 7. 6. 5. 4. 3. 2. 1.

Question 8

QUIZMASTER:

In many countries, there is a common saying that "if cats lick themselves, fair weather comes". Scientists have observed that cats do, in fact, tend to lick their fur more often when humidity is low, which is often a precursor to fine weather. Why do cats do this? Is it because:

(a) damp fur helps cats to cool off in warm weather

(b) cats prefer not to clean themselves in cold weather

(c) cat fur builds up static electricity in low humidity, which can irritate cats?

TIMEKEEPER:

(waits until 20 seconds have passed, then counts down the last ten seconds):

10. 9. 8. 7. 6. 5. 4. 3. 2. 1.

Question 9

QUIZMASTER:

And now for the final question of the quiz. In many countries around the world, the behaviour of animals is traditionally used as a predictor of weather and the seasons. As this quiz has indicated, many sayings from folklore do, in fact, have a scientific basis.

One of the more well-known animal prediction events takes place in the northern hemisphere in winter, on 2 February each year. In the USA, this popular tradition is known as Groundhog Day.

A groundhog is a type of ground-dwelling squirrel. Tradition has it that if a groundhog emerges from its burrow on 2 February and sees its shadow, another six weeks of harsh winter weather can be expected.

In northern Europe, a similar saying is applied to badgers and hedgehogs. In southern and central Europe, the occurrence of bears emerging from hibernation is traditionally used as a weather predictor.

Question 9 is: how accurate is a groundhog in predicting how much longer winter will last? Is it:

(a) wrong more times than it is right

(b) right more times than it is wrong

(c) equally right or wrong around half the time?

TIMEKEEPER:

(waits until 20 seconds have passed, then counts down the last ten seconds):

10. 9. 8. 7. 6. 5. 4. 3. 2. 1.

That's the end of the third and final round. All team scribes must hand in their answers to the scrutineer now.

(Once all teams have handed in their answer sheets, the adjudicator stands. While the quizmaster and the adjudicator are giving the following answers, the scrutineer counts up the correct answers for each team, adds them to the scores for rounds one and two and records the final results on the whiteboard.)

a groundhog

QUIZMASTER:

Answer to question 7: Is it possible to work out the exact temperature by listening to a cricket chirping?

ADJUDICATOR:

Yes, it is.

The speed at which a cricket chirps is directly related to the temperature. To work out the temperature in degrees Celsius, count the number of times a cricket chirps in 25 seconds. Divide that number by 3, and then add 4. The answer will equate to the exact temperature in degrees Celsius.

a cricket

This situation occurs because crickets, like all insects, are cold-blooded. Temperature directly affects the rate at which chemical reactions can occur within a cricket's body – such as the chemical reactions needed to make muscles twitch. As temperatures increase, more chemical reactions (and therefore twitches) can take place. Scientists describe this phenomenon using a complex chemical formula called the Arrhenius Equation, which correlates the two exactly.

Folklore Fact

a cicada

The Symbol of Summer

In Japanese culture, the song of the cicada is celebrated as symbolic of summer's arrival. In Java, Indonesia, farmers traditionally saw the first songs of the cicada as a sign that the dry season had begun and they should plant non-rice crops.

Why does a cicada song mark the start of hot and dry weather? The cicada makes its characteristic clicking song by bending a hard shell-like membrane inwards and outwards. When the weather is wet, the membrane becomes too soft to "click", and therefore a cicada cannot sing. The cicada can only make a noise when the weather is dry!

QUIZMASTER:

Answer to question 8: Why do cats lick their fur more often when humidity is low?

ADJUDICATOR:

When humidity is low, a cat's fine fur becomes much more susceptible to a build-up of static electricity. A cat may actively avoid rubbing itself up against fabric-covered furniture or being stroked during these times, as a discharge of static electricity can create unpleasant sparks, or electric shocks, to the cat's skin.

Cats lick their fur more frequently in times of low humidity because static electricity is more easily dissipated through damp fur.

The answer is (c): cat fur builds up static electricity in low humidity, which can irritate cats.

A Leopard Never Changes Its Spots

The saying "a leopard never changes its spots", which means that some people's behaviour always remains the same, is not scientifically true. A baby leopard's spots change in shape and colour as they grow into adults.

Each leopard has its own unique pattern, in the same way that no two sets of human fingerprints are identical.

QUIZMASTER:

Answer to question 9: How accurate is a groundhog in predicting how much longer winter will last?

ADJUDICATOR:

Despite most of the traditional sayings and folklore we've examined here having some scientific basis, the tradition of Groundhog Day in the USA has been shown to be wrong at least 60 per cent of the time. In Canada, where Groundhog Day is also popular, groundhogs are even worse at predicting how much longer wintry weather will last. They get it wrong about 66 per cent of the time!

The answer, unfortunately for groundhogs, is (a): they get it wrong more times than they get it right.

Folklore Fact

The Early Bird Catches the Worm

The saying "the early bird catches the worm", which means that people who start their daily tasks early in the morning will be more successful than those who start them later, has been scientifically proven to be true.

A study by German biologists in 2012 showed that people whose biorhythms were adjusted to perform well in the mornings tended to be more proactive, were more successful at school and had better jobs as adults. Those people whose biorhythms peaked in the afternoons were shown to be less organised, but more creative.

QUIZMASTER:

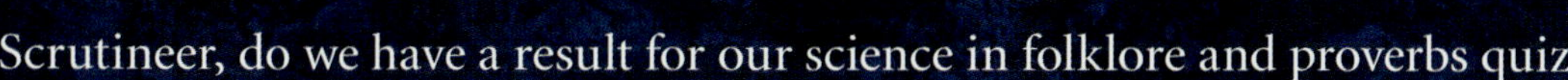

Scrutineer, do we have a result for our science in folklore and proverbs quiz?

SCRUTINEER:

Yes, we do.

In third place, we have: *(announces team in third place).*

In second place, we have: *(announces team in second place).*

And, in first place, the team with the most correct answers, is: *(announces team in first place).*

QUIZMASTER:

Can we please have a round of applause for all the teams?

Well done, everybody. We hope you've enjoyed participating in this fun quiz, and learned some interesting science facts along the way! But, here's the best news – the twist in the tale!

ADJUDICATOR:

Who'd like another quiz?

Throughout this book, there have been lots of interesting fact boxes about other traditional sayings, folklore and proverbs, some of which have a scientific basis and some of which do not.

TIMEKEEPER:

The challenge to the winning team is to arrange a time with their teacher and classmates to hold another quiz, just like this one, using questions and answers that they find in the fact boxes in these pages.

Folklore Fact

They'll set the questions, and this time, they'll be the quizmaster, timekeeper, adjudicator and scrutineer.

SCRUTINEER:

Students may also find other science questions and answers they think are interesting or challenging. They may find facts or figures they think are quirky or unusual. They may just want to use the information from this book. And whichever team wins the next quiz might want to have a go at running the following one! But, whatever happens, there's one important thing to remember.

QUIZMASTER ADJUDICATOR TIMEKEEPER SCRUTINEER *(all together)*:

HAVE FUN!

SOME SAMPLE QUESTIONS FOR THE NEXT QUIZ

Why are some clouds called nimbus clouds? Is it because they are:

(a) fast-moving and nimble

(b) named after the Latin word for "raincloud"

(c) easily spotted from a school bus?

Why are we told to "strike while the iron is hot"? Is it because:

(a) creases are more easily removed when clothes are repeatedly hit with a hot iron

(b) people prefer not to be struck with cold iron objects

(c) time is of the essence when you're shaping a horseshoe?

If someone is described as long in the tooth, does it mean they are:

(a) old

(b) in need of some cosmetic dentistry

(c) wearing a vampire costume for Halloween?

Just my luck ... first again!
I knew I should've stayed in bed.

Some people say "the early bird catches the worm, but the second mouse gets the cheese". Does this mean:

(a) the first mouse is too busy watching for birds and worms

(b) not being the first to try something can be a good thing

(c) no one puts out cheese until mid morning?

THINK UP SOME MORE QUIRKY QUESTIONS OF YOUR OWN!

Index

Glossary

adjudicator A person who acts as a judge in a competition or argument, and makes a formal decision about the results

Arrhenius Equation A simple formula that shows the relationship between the rate of a chemical reaction and its temperature

biorhythm A regular pattern of physical processes in an organism, that can influence moods and behaviour

folklore A traditional story or belief

proverb A short saying that gives advice or makes a comment about life

scrutineer A person who examines the counting of votes or scores to make sure the counting has been done correctly

static electricity An electrical charge that collects on the surface of objects, created when two surfaces come into contact and separate